Buffy
THE VAMPIRE SLAYER™
BAD BLOOD

Buffy THE VAMPIRE SLAYER™
BAD BLOOD

based on the television series created by
JOSS WHEDON

writer ANDI WATSON

penciller JOE BENNET

inker RICK KETCHAM

colorist GUY MAJOR

letterer JANICE CHIANG

and featuring "Hello, Moon"
written by CHRISTOPHER GOLDEN and DANIEL BRERETON

penciller JOE BENNET

inker JIM AMASH

colorist GUY MAJOR

letterer CLEM ROBINS

These stories take place during Buffy the Vampire Slayer's third season.

Titan Books

publisher
MIKE RICHARDSON

editor
SCOTT ALLIE
with ADAM GALLARDO *and* BEN ABERNATHY

collection designer
KEITH WOOD

art director
MARK COX

special thanks to
DEBBIE OLSHAN AT FOX LICENSING,
CAROLINE KALLAS AND GEORGE SNYDER AT *BUFFY THE VAMPIRE SLAYER*,
AND DAVID CAMPITI AT GLASS HOUSE GRAPHICS.

PUBLISHED BY
TITAN BOOKS
144 SOUTHWARK STREET
LONDON SE1 0UP

what did you think of this book? we love to hear from our readers.
please e-mail us at readerfeedback@titanemail.com or write to
Reader Feedback at the address above.

FIRST EDITION
MAY 2000
ISBN: 1-84023-179-3

3 5 7 9 10 8 6 4 2

printed in italy by valprint

introduction

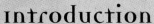

Last fall, just months after Angel's return from Hell, Buffy Summers' holidays were ruined by a new vampire in town—the beautiful Selke. On Halloween a group of bloodsuckers kidnapped Willow Rosenburg. When Buffy came for her best friend, only Selke escaped, spared by an off-the-mark stake from the Slayer. On Thanksgiving Selke returned, much worse for wear, and managed to take Buffy captive. Buffy got out by the skin of her teeth after setting fire to the rotted wood and scattered coffins of Selke's mausoleum home, leaving the wounded vampire to die in flames …*

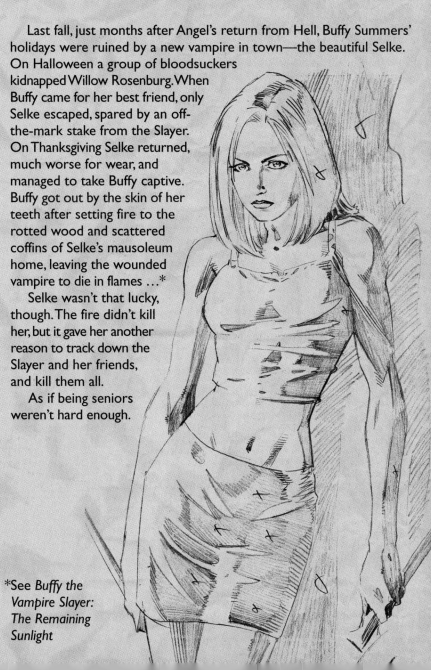

Selke wasn't that lucky, though. The fire didn't kill her, but it gave her another reason to track down the Slayer and her friends, and kill them all.

As if being seniors weren't hard enough.

*See *Buffy the Vampire Slayer: The Remaining Sunlight*

Art by JEFF MATSUDA and JON SIBAL
Colors by LIQUID!

HEY, GOOD LOOKIN'

PART 1

BIP BIP BIP

BIP BIP BIP

MISTRESS SELKE?

BIP BIP BIP

YOU ORDERED OUT? HOW SWEET.

BIP BEEP BEEEP SUCK SCHLUP

BEEEE EEEEEP

I'VE FOUND MY APPETITE--

--AND BUFFY'S NEXT ON THE MENU

HEY, GOOD LOOKIN'

PART II

YOU WANT A FACE-LIFT? YOU'VE COME TO THE RIGHT PLACE.

SCHLUP SCHLUP.

...HAT WAS MY LAST ...TIENT, MISTRESS. ...VON'T BE ABLE ...NVITE ANY MORE ...OR TREATMENT, ... AFTER YOU ATE ...Y RECEPTIONIST.

SMARTEN YOURSELF UP, DOC. I'M GONNA TAKE YOU OUT TO MEET THE RELATIVES.

YOU HAVE A FAMILY?

I'M NOT QUITE MYSELF YET. I CAN'T HANDLE THE SLAYER WITHOUT A LITTLE HELP FROM THE OLD GANG.

NOW CHANGE THAT OLD COAT, YOU LOOK A MESS.

Art by JEFF MATSUDA and JON SIBAL
Colors by GUY MAJOR

A BOY
NAMED SUE

WE'RE CALLED [DOU]BLE-CROSS AND [W]E'RE HEADLINING [TH]E BRONZE TONIGHT. [C]ATCH US NOW, [B]EFORE WE'RE ALL OVER MTV.

BUFFY SUMMERS, RIGHT? I DON'T THINK WE'VE EVER MET.

LET ME GUESS, THE LEAD SINGER OF DOUBLE-CROSS?

TODD DAHL, A PLEASURE TO MEET YOU. SO, YOU WANNA COME SEE MY BAND TONIGHT? I'LL PUT YOU RIGHT ON TOP OF THE GUEST LIST.

NO PROBS. I'M ALREADY THERE. MY FRIEND OZ IS PLAYING TONIGHT.

THAT'S RIGHT. DINGOES ARE WARMING UP FOR US.

SO YOU'LL BE HOT WHEN I HIT THE STAGE?

IF THE A/C'S WRECKED.

DAHL, TODD?

THAT'S MY CALL. SEE YOU TONIGHT.

WILL'S NOT IN A DANCING MOOD?

SHE'S SHOWING BOYFRIEND SOLIDARITY BY IGNORING THE HEADLINERS.

SO WHAT'S THE DEAL WITH THE BLOOD BANK?

I'M ON CALL. GILES'LL BE IN TOUCH IF IT LOOKS LIKE TROUBLE.

JUST LIKE "E.R." ONLY YOU IMPALE THE SICK INSTEAD OF CURING THEM.

CORDY, ABOUT YOUR BEDSIDE MANNER?

TODD! WOULD YOU PLEASE--

-- SIGN...?

GLAD YOU COULD MAKE IT. DID YOU LIKE THE SET?

YEAH, IT WAS FINE.

I SAW YOU DANCING OUT THERE, YOU LOOKED GREAT.

THANKS. MY FRIENDS ARE WAITING.

YOU BLEW THOSE GUYS AWAY, OZ.

TRUE, THEY'RE ALL STYLE OVER SUBSTANCE.

...THOUGHT MAYBE WE'D EAT, Y'KNOW SOMEWHERE QUIET, WHERE WE COULD TALK.

I APPRECIATE THE OFFER, BUT NO THANKS.

A DRINK THEN, LET ME--

TAKE A HINT, TODD.

EVEN IF I DIDN'T HAVE A BOYFRIEND I WOULDN'T BE INTERESTED, SO QUIT THE TOUCHY-FEELY STUFF. OKAY?

ANGTHHH!

BLEEP BLEEP!

THAT'S MY CALL.

SURE, I'LL...MEET YOU, LATER.

WHAT'S HIS DAMAGE?

¿Heh¿ WON'T BE PLAYING ANY BAR CHORDS FOR AWHILE.

BLEEP BLEEP.

HI, TODD. MY NAME'S AMY--

ARE YOU STILL HERE?! LEMME GUESS-- ONE OF THE DINGOES ORDERED A STALKER FOR ME AS A JOKE!

--SO SHE COMES RUNNING OUT OF THE CAN HOLDING THESE BAGGY PANTS UP--

--NO MAKEUP, HER HAIR JUST ALL OVER THE PLACE--

--WHATEVER! I MEAN, IF YOU'RE GONNA GO INTO THE BOY'S BATHROOM, PUT SOMETHING DECENT ON!

--HIT THE ROOF WHEN SHE HEARD TODD HAD TOLD EVERY--

WHOA, TRENT-- WHAT'S THE HUBBUB?

THE NEW GIRL GOT CAUGHT RUNNING OUT OF THE BOYS' BATHROOM.

NEW GIRL?

YEAH, RIGHT OVER THERE. SHE SEEMS NICE AND EVERYTHING, BUT I MEAN, DRESSED LIKE THAT, HANGING OUT IN THE BOYS' BATHROOM-- DEFINITELY LOOSE.

SO IT WAS A MISTAKE GOING IN THERE, AND IF YOU JUST LET ME OFF THIS ONE TIME, I--

HEY, GUYS! I THINK SHE'S CHECKING YOU OUT!

YOU GUYS HAVE TO HELP ME-- YOU'RE NEVER GOING TO BELIEVE--

WHO WHO SLO DOW BAE

Art by JOE BENNETT
Colors by GUY MAJOR

HELLO MOON

HELLO MOON

IT'S ME, BUFFY. IT'S NICE TO JUST ...SEE YOU,

SHOULD BE TROLLING. I [K]NOW THAT. THAT [LIT]TLE GUILT [VO]ICE IN MY HEAD [T]HE ONE THAT [SO]UNDS SUSPI- [CIO]USLY LIKE [GI]LES? IT'S A [CO]NSTANT [R]EMINDER.

BUT I CUT PATROL SHORT TONIGHT. I JUST NEEDED SOME TIME FOR MYSELF. I JUST NEEDED TO WATCH THE WAVES AND SMELL THE OCEAN AND STARE AT THE MOON.

I NEEDED TO GET AWAY.

YEAH...

HRRRR...

...RIGHT.

WHAT IN THE... HEY!